POEMS BY NANCY WOOD

PAINTINGS BY FRANK HOWELL

A Doubleday Book for Young Readers

SHAMAN'S
CIRCLE

Published by
Delacorte Press
Bantam Doubleday Dell Publishing Group, Inc.
1540 Broadway
New York, New York 10036

Doubleday and the portrayal of an anchor with a dolphin
are trademarks of Bantam Doubleday Dell Publishing Group, Inc.

Library of Congress Cataloging-in-Publication Data
Wood, Nancy C.
    The shaman's circle : poems by Nancy Wood ; paintings by Frank
Howell.
        p.   cm.
    Summary: Poetry and paintings follow the cycles of nature and
human life as seen through the traditional beliefs and rituals of
the Taos Indians of the American Southwest.
    ISBN 0-385-32222-4 (hc : alk. paper)
    1. Taos Indians—Juvenile poetry.   2. Children's poetry, American.
[1. Taos Indians—Poetry.   2. Indians of North America—Southwest,
New—Poetry.   3. American poetry.]   I. Howell, Frank, ill.
II. Title.
PS3573.0595S53   1996
811'.54—dc20   95-52387
                                                    CIP
                                                    AC

Manufactured in the United States of America

The text of this book is set in 15-point Centaur.

Book design by Patrice Sheridan

October 1996

10 9 8 7 6 5 4 3 2 1

For Robert W. Parker

Campfire

More than thirty years ago, I visited Taos Pueblo for the first time. It was a clear, cold March morning, with the snow-capped Sangre de Cristo Mountains towering above the six-hundred-year-old adobe village. The north and south villages were separated by a swiftly flowing river, ice still clinging to its edges; there women gathered water in clay jars, the way they'd done for centuries, and in metal buckets, a modern touch. As I watched those women in long, homemade skirts and high-topped white buckskin boots stooping toward the dark, rushing water, they began to sing back and forth to one another. I realized that this simple ritual had been going on for centuries.

I inhaled deeply, smelling the sweet juniper smoke curling from numerous pueblo chimneys. In 1961, most of the population of Taos Pueblo lived inside the ancient walled village; few people had automobiles. Horse-drawn wagons, piled high with wood gathered from the mountains, lined the plaza. Women were baking bread in their *hornos,* or ovens, dozens of loaves at a time, and these they lifted out with long wooden paddles. Around the plaza, drying racks held long strips of venison. I began to walk slowly along the river, thinking how easily the Indians made rituals of everyday life. Why couldn't we?

Suddenly half a dozen men, wrapped like mummies in tight-fitting cotton blankets, appeared on the rooftops, crying to one another in their native Tiwa language. They were, I learned later, the town criers, and several times a day they called out news to the people: it might have been about the death of an elder or the birth of a child, the coming of spring, or the summoning of important men to the kiva. Time seemed to stand still as I climbed the ladder to the second-story pueblo home of Ben Marcus, the forceful Pueblo religious leader who, through his lifetime position, exerted great power over his tribe. I sat in the cool, dim interior of his simple home, eating a bowl of venison stew and freshly baked bread offered by his wife, Manuelita, who wore buckskin moccasins and a homemade cotton print dress that hung to her ankles. If I closed my eyes, I could imagine myself in the fourteenth century, when the mud house I was sitting in had been built by Ben's ancestors, more than twenty generations before.

On that day, past, present, and future blended into one continuous circle of life, like the ripples caused by tossing a handful of pebbles into a pond. I felt something sacred and profound happening. This sacred circle is, I later learned, an ancient, revered means of passing wisdom from generation to generation, through storytelling, ritual, and common sharing by like-minded people. The Indians call this sacred knowledge the shaman's circle; it embodies the highest form of respect for the living world. In essence, the shaman's circle lies at the very core of Pueblo Indian belief.

Ben Marcus figured prominently in the shaman's circle of his tribe. He was a wise and respected leader who, over the next twenty years, shared with me deep insights that affected my life from that day on. Eventually, I began to find my own circles, created my own rituals, and learned that we non-Indians can, in a limited way, absorb the sacred knowledge of the complex living world.

Again and again I returned to Taos Pueblo, even after Ben Marcus died in 1983. I attended dances for harvest, for rain, for thanksgiving, for the continuation of the tribe. I watched a newborn baby being plunged into the icy waters of the river, in a purification ritual that includes naming by elders. One bleak, cold November morning I attended the burial of an aged Indian friend, whose blanket-wrapped body was carried from the church by six men, each holding one end of the stout ropes tied securely around the body. My friend's moccasined feet dangled limply from the blanket. As we walked along from the church to the cemetery, the grieving relatives began to sing. As soon as the burial was over, with gifts of food, water, and fetishes gently tucked around his body and dirt heaped on his grave by family members, the old man's personal belongings were gathered up and destroyed before the sun set. Eyeglasses. Clothing. A cane. Blankets. Even his favorite coffee mug. Pueblo Indians believe that the belongings of the dead must be destroyed in order to ensure safe passage into the next world.

Then the Indian women prepared a feast of the dead man's favorite dishes, which they left along the riverbanks for him to eat whenever he got hungry: *posole,* chili, fresh bread, apple pie, a thick, rich stew. It smelled delicious. The next day, the plates were licked clean. "Could it be animals?" I asked. "Oh, no," one of my friends replied, "he was very hungry. He ate everything." For the next three days, everyone went quietly around the village; they seemed to be waiting for something. I was told that during this period the dead person roams the pueblo, playing tricks on friends and family.

I also witnessed several Pueblo weddings, performed in native costume by a tribal elder in natural surroundings. I helped at feast days when great mountains of food, lovingly prepared, were offered to all who came through the door, part of the old Pueblo tradition of hospitality. Once I helped gather sacred micaceous clay in the mountains with a Taos potter, watching her offer cornmeal, sage, and tobacco to the spirits so that her pots would be strong. I observed a ceremony in which an elder takes a long stick and digs a hole in the moist earth and drops in the first corn seeds. This is called planting Mother Earth's Navel, one of the oldest springtime rituals anywhere on earth. Another time, an old Indian woman taught me how to feed the spirits, when we were on a picnic in the mountains. She broke off a piece of bread and dropped it on the ground. Then she poured out a cup of water. The spirits were always hungry and thirsty, she told me. Ever since that day, I have observed this particular ritual myself.

One bitter cold Christmas Day I stood in the plaza, slightly taken aback, as a holy man placed a "communion" of tiny pieces of raw deer meat on the tongues of the weary dancers. They chewed this meat slowly, and it seemed to replenish them. Once, when I was privileged to spend the night in the pueblo, I was awakened by the sounds of two different groups of men, who were singing and drumming on the bridges over the river, to keep it company so that it would not dry up. Another morning, I was awakened from a sound sleep on the floor of a pueblo apartment by a long, shrill cry. I jumped up to see a man standing on a rooftop, arms outstretched to greet the sun. His joyous song was returned by men on other pueblo rooftops. (Ben Marcus once explained that if a man did not greet the sun each morning, it would fall back into the underworld.) Another time, when I was so sick I thought I was going to die, a Pueblo medicine woman came to my house with her herbs and her curing chants, and soon my fever disappeared.

The Pueblo world, unlike our own, revolves entirely around ritual, a major part of the shaman's circle. Tribes observe rituals for seasons, equinoxes, and solstices; hunting rituals are part of tribal life; so are puberty rites, manhood rites (in the kivas), and marriage rites. The very act of life itself is a ritual, from birth to death and beyond. To the Pueblo Indians, death is only a change of worlds; heaven and hell are here and now, and they are of one's own making.

In Pueblo cosmology, animals deserve rituals too. There are dances for the bear, deer, turtle, eagle, snake, and butterfly, all of which are sacred beings, responsible for the well-being and education of the people. These dances are performed as part of a rigorous belief system that requires the blessing and approval of animal, corn, and cloud spirits for the people to survive. The Indians blame sickness, famine, and death on their failure to conduct their rituals properly, which in turn means that individual and tribal obligations have not been met.

For hundreds of thousands of years, ritual has been a necessary part of human life the world over. It is the basis of all religion, essential to harmony, continuity, and mystery. Rituals explain the inexplicable; they strengthen community ties; they open the individual to connections with others and to self-evaluation. They are affirmation of the highest sort. Through ritual, the Indians have preserved what is essential in their everyday lives, be it a simple act of grinding corn or making pottery. Reverence is the key to every act. For this, ritual is necessary.

Indian lives are steeped in sacred ceremony, centered around the seasons. In summer, for instance, Pueblos hold one or more Corn Dances, which honor not only a crop that used to provide sustenance for these people, but what many believe is the means by which they traveled from the underworld—a sacred cornstalk that brought them out of darkness into light. Corn provided the first food; its tassels were paths to knowledge; its stalk led deep into the earth, while its ears were an offering to the sky. A major fall ritual is harvest; in the old days, a poor harvest meant starvation, so the people were careful that the rituals for the growing season—and the time-honored methods of gathering corn—were respectfully observed. Winter rituals consisted of praying for the sun to return from its long journey to the south; animals were acknowledged during this period, as were the migrating birds. Spring rituals were centered around homage to Mother Earth, offering prayers for rain and for the purification of the human spirit.

Most of us non-Indians are out of touch with the magic of the seasons, the subtle rhythms of the earth, and the daily blessings of the natural world. We hardly notice birds building nests, green leaves budding, or the way a river swells with life in spring. We are too busy to care. But care we must, for we are inextricably tied to nature, and to one another. We have to rediscover ritual and, in so doing, rediscover ourselves. We need to strengthen our bonds with nature, every day of the year. Few of us greet the rising sun or bid it farewell at sunset; not many of us howl at the moon, nor do we sing to rainclouds, growing corn, or the death spirit. We have drifted away from our roots, and melancholy prevails. Now we must reestablish contact with our sacred center and invent rituals that have personal meaning.

These poems are a ritual in themselves. They're meant to be read in private, preferably under a tree or beside a stream. They're meant to trigger a desire to get up and dance. Or to sing. Or to write a poem of your own as you enter the shaman's sacred circle, where anything can happen.

Nancy Wood
Santa Fe, New Mexico
November 1995

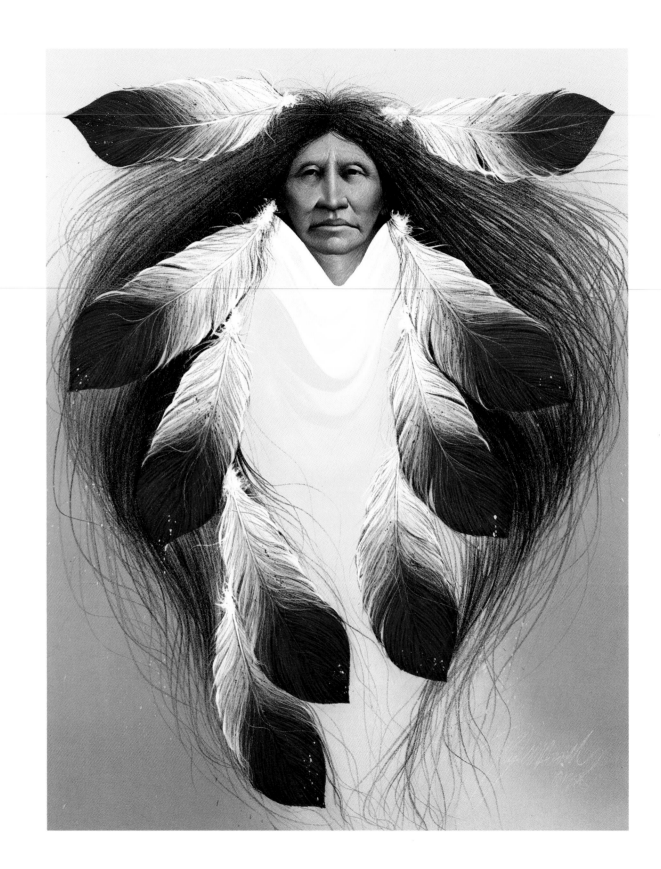

Pink Rose

SHAMAN'S CIRCLE

Inside the shaman's circle lie the feathers of peace and
the ashes of battle, each one essential to our task
of remembering how mankind's continuing thread
knits up light and dark, without discernment.

Inside the shaman's circle lie songs as well as tears,
for laughter diminishes the pain of hopelessness,
and springtime's kiss makes the claws of winter
bearable. The shaman's circle is a fiery wheel

Of opposites necessary for the world to keep on
turning, and for migrating birds to remember
how to build nests, and for fish to reclaim the
place of their birth. Within this circle, nothing dies.

The shaman's circle encompasses the stars, and beyond them,
the shadow of creation, so vast it touches children
yet unborn, so significant it lines the paths of ancestors,
who struggle in their silence to tell us
how melting ice becomes a raging river,
in time.

Turquoise Dissolution

BEGINNING TIME

The beginning of each new day means
    that I am born anew into a world
Where hatred, fear, and jealousy vanish on a tongue
    of hope licking away sorrow and despair.

The magpie and the prairie dog lead me toward
    the rising Sun. In its holy path I see
The embryo face of time's child, telling me that
    youth's determination to unlearn the lessons
Of an impoverished world is given strength at dawn.

The middle years of life's long afternoon promise
    nothing more than summer every year.
The jealous shadows of yesterday are merely tomorrow's old men,
    resisting the knuckles of old age.

In the beginning time of such overlapping generations
    lies the indistinct history of restless skeletons.
Listen! They are singing the songs of children and embryos.
    They are preparing the earth for you to dance upon.

WHEN THE MORNINGSTARS
SANG TOGETHER

In the old, dark days of the Beginning Time, nothing
    had a voice. The echo of silence rolled
Across the dry void of the Universe, no presence except for
    a Male and a Female Star, so far apart not even
The spirits were heard by them. Sky was hungry
    for the fist of fire, also for cleansing winds
    and fresh rain, birds, and the power of mystery.

When Earth sank down, Sky lifted up, and both
    Sun and Moon were born. The Milky Way formed a web
Of far-extending potential, while on Earth, seas and
    mountains emerged from rainbow mist. Drifting night
And abiding day came about at the same time leaves grew
    and died on trees. But there were no animals or fish,
    no snakes or insects or inquisitive turtles.

When the emerging light of First Dawn brought together
    the Male and the Female Stars, they discovered
The delight of song. This was the First Harmony and
    the First Unity, the Supreme Connection of the Great
Hanging Space of the Universe. When the Morningstars
    sang together, the heartbeat of the Earth began,
    and in the Sky, the oldest hunger
    was satisfied.

SPRING: BRINGING THE BUDS TO LIFE

Listen! In the earth, the seeds are stirring and making noise,
    like the birds whose song has been silenced by winter. Now
    the snow is being devoured by sun our elder and in the branches,
The persistence of our prayers is bringing the buds to life.

September Prayer

THE SACRED SONGS OF
OUR ANCESTORS

When people first emerged into the world, it was a sacred time
    because humans and animals were able to talk to one another.
All things had a voice, even the pottery which our women made
    from clay gathered from a sacred spot where the earth
Reminded them to pay attention to blossoms and smoke, so that

The pottery would be strong. When a man took a rock and from it made
    the sacred shape of an obsidian point, he spoke to the stone.
And the stone answered back. Without dialogue, stones would
    not become arrowheads, and we would not eat, for
it is impossible to take the life of an animal without the power of stone.

In those days we spoke with life and thus knew beauty all around.
    In our pottery and carvings, weavings and weapons,
We brought forth the essence of the Creator. When animals spoke,
it was to teach us valuable lessons. When the Clay Mother permitted
women to gather her sacred earth, we were blessed. The sacred songs

Of our ancestors still echo today. Who has the courage to listen?

Dakota Skies

THE PATH

Whatever you become, my child, may it be rooted in grace.
Whatever your path through life,
may it offer you steepness and rough places, so that you do not become
complacent. Nothing is owed to you, but everything is available to you,

Even the decision to do nothing and to travel nowhere.
It's up to you to decide
whether to follow the wisdom of our ancestors, or to pursue
the cheap solutions of the world. Your courage will arise

If you call it by name, just as love will find its way into your heart, in time.
My child, I cannot shoulder your mistakes
in order to keep you free from pain,
but I can open your eyes to beauty, if you will only take the time.

PUBERTY

The first blood of womanhood means that you can now begin
    to carry the seed of the farthest star, my daughter,
    and borrow from oceans the fecundity of whales. From your
Breasts a molten heat arises and in its cooling you will discover
    the roots of all our being. Without you, my daughter,
    the world would perish and the music of womanhood

Would become the silence of despair. Oh, my daughter,
    Go forth in harmony, wearing your gown of anticipation.
    Remember that you and you alone must decide whether
The fruit of your womb shall ripen with unborn children,
    Or if in its silence your richness shall contain itself.
    The future is up to you, my daughter. Embrace the opportunity
To become the woman who holds up her half of the sky.

THE MARRIAGE OF STARS AND FLOWERS

When stars first appeared in the sky, they were lonely, never
    touching, or becoming touched by what lay beyond their isolation.
    They had deep eyes with which to examine the sinews of
The universe and secret ears with which to hear the struggling whispers
    of plants emerging from the earth below. After a while,
    when the stars were looking within themselves for meaning,

They noticed a field of yellow flowers swaying in the wind of a
    distant mountaintop. These flowers were patient and unresisting,
    some so small that the stars couldn't see them very well,
But they knew these living things to be mirrors of their own vast beauty.
    Thus stars married flowers in loving affirmation
Of one another, expecting nothing more than recognition
    of their unimportant differences.

Insight

BIRTH RITUAL

New being, new citizen of the world, new carrier
    of cloud wisdom and moonstones, new
    flame of the universe, new eyes of animals
    too old to see beyond their footprints, new repetition
Of the old ideas that people thought had died long ago,
    we stand before you, ready to protect your small
    breath of life, ready to teach you songs, ready to
    help you plow the fields cluttered with our mistakes. Your
Recent journey affirms our faith in ancient circles. You are
    the voice of us who tried to change the world. You are
    the continuity of seasons and migrations, the best
    or worst of all that has gone before. New being,
The ancestors are depending on you to surprise them. Little one,
    our prayers for you come with love and heartbreak.
    The world you enter is dangerous and filled with
    imbalance. Knowledge comes from experience, not from
Easy answers. Resist those who would have you blindly follow them,
    dear child of buffalo and hawks, ladybugs and fireflies. Turn instead
    to the rhythm of waves, the pattern of grass, the shape of clouds,
    the music of raindrops, and the color of autumn leaves. Strong
Mountains and saplings await you. The tongues of animals are anxious
    to speak to you and the river is eager to teach you to dance. Learn
    from the vagaries of winds, the honking of geese, the dance
    of trembling leaves, and the way that shadows mystify.
New being, this is all you will need to be at home in the world.
New being, this is all you will need to recognize your song.

Crow Owner

THE MEANING OF DAYLIGHT

Daylight is an interval of changing shadows and long vision,
    when stars and moon are swallowed up by the strong fist
    of Father Sun, there to bargain for release
Into the completed paths of dead bodies in the universe.

Daylight's insistence on survival results in corn forests
    and in clouds of blossoms, where ancient people rest,
    remembering purifying smoke and comforting food,
Offered for the satisfaction of more than ordinary hunger.

Daylight is nighttime's other face, the one that preceded
    creation and formed a universal vision long before
    human eyes recognized the lessons of leaves and lions.

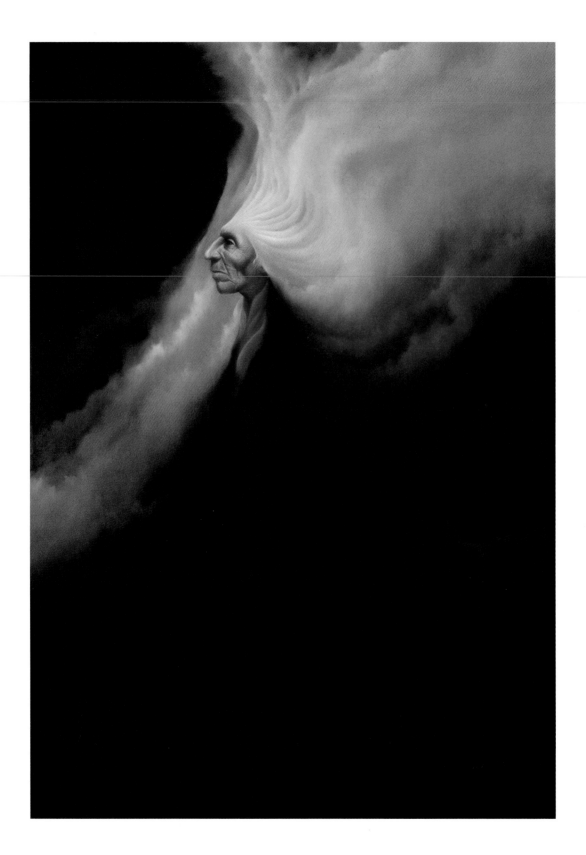

Father's Sweet Storm

THE OLD WAYS

The old ways are the ways of northern geese
    with tired wings piercing the thrust
of instinct, expanding to connect their flight
    to ancient ice and the blank inquiry of snow.

The old ways are the ways of sacred buffalo,
    frantic to escape a bullet death that
made false heroes out of ordinary men
    who laid waste nature's intricate web.

The old ways are the ways of spruce trees
    connecting earth to sky, ladders to
The sun's fitful isolation and the curiosity
    Of stars embedded in the hair of god.

The old ways are the ways of unmoving stones
    scattered like knowledge across life's path,
Waiting to be noticed, or perhaps taught to speak
    the language of geese and trees and buffalo.

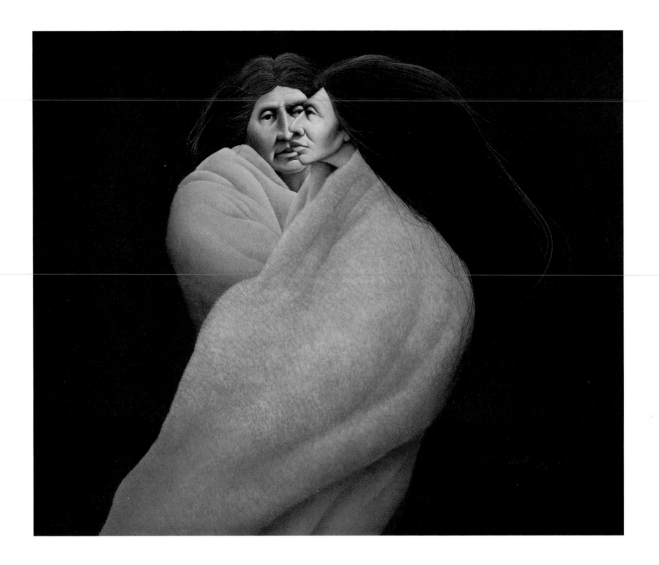

Silent Whispers

SACRED LOVE: A RITUAL

Enduring heart of a man accustomed to lying down with stars
and walking where grizzly bears watch the shadows you
cast, even in the rain, I feel the beat of you asserting
the strength that mountains need in order to survive.

In this high meadow, where a stream carries our fears away,
I weave you a ring of grass and between your toes I plant
summer's brightest flowers. Your laughter commands the sun
to move and in your eyes is reflected the swift blessing

Of an eagle who understands our desire to be joined. The circles
you make of cornmeal and tobacco are offerings
for the spirits who protect us here in this sacred place,
where our sacred love has finally found a home.

PUEBLO WISDOM

A hard-hearted man will reap stones, while a jealous woman will spit out
thorns, and in her heart a snake will lay its eggs. A man who cheats others
betrays himself, and in his eyes you will see dead fires reflected. Put aside

your vanity and become the person you are afraid of becoming. Don't
listen to half-truths; they will poison the river of your mind. Turn your back
on those who would steal your heart, for they will want your skeleton too.

The measure of a warrior or a wise woman is how well
each survives life's storms without complaining. The gifts of a warrior
or a wise woman are the songs captured by the tongue of wind
when the music ends, and no one dances, anymore.

GATHERING LIFE'S TOOLS

From my grandmother I learned courage, the kind needed
    to fight for what I believe in. From my grandfather
I learned patience, the winter he went hungry so that
    our family could eat. From both of them I learned to care
For the smallest things, unnoticed until one learns to see
    beyond the cluttered path. Corn commanded me to listen
    to its growth and the field mouse took me along
    on its journey to new horizons. My life was hard and my body ached
    from doing the work of a man when I was only a boy. My home
    was simple, yet it contained the riches of a king, for love flowed

Like the river that sang me to sleep each night. From my mother I learned
    tenderness, the value of laughter, the importance of concern. From my
    father I learned how to hunt in the mountains and how to speak to the
    deer about his death. Among my people I was given the opportunity
To listen to stories passed down through the ages and exchange
    self-importance for wisdom. In solitude I found solace whenever I asked
    to be comforted, and in the wilderness I found mystery.

I gathered life's tools carefully, one by one. Now that I am a man,
    I know life's most important lessons came from those
    who recognized my ignorance, and merely called it youth.

Grandmother's Whispers

FEATHER

The bluebird and I were friends, the kind that depend on one another
   to reaffirm life's patterns and to embrace the cleansing wind.
He awakened me with a song each morning and in his voice I recognized
   his wider experience of rising above difficulty to reach
The purity of clouds and wind and sun. In my garden I offered him
   water and seed and acceptance, never knowing if he understood
My simple gifts were meant to praise him. Then one day upon the ground
   I noticed a single bluebird feather. What deeper gift can a bird
Give than what enables him to fly? Or to sing the song of his creation
   to me, forever rooted to the ground?

SUMMER: THE CORN FINDS ITS OWN LIFE

Believe our old ways.
Within them is the saving of the world through repetition
of stories and dances that we have known forever. We in our longevity
have helped the corn find its own life for as many years as the sun
Has crossed the sky alone, believing it would reach the other side,
eventually.

COMMITMENT

Before we met, you and I were halves unjoined except
 in the wide rivers of our minds. We were each other's
Distant shore, the opposite wings of birds, the other half
 of a shell that keeps the clam from falling out.
We did not know each other then, did not know our determination
 to keep alive the cry of one riverbank to the other.
We were apart, yet connected in our ignorance of each other,
 like two apples sharing a common tree. Remember?

I knew you existed long before you understood my desire
 to join my loneliness to yours. Our paths
Collided long enough for our indecision to be swallowed up
 by the greater needs of love. When you came to me,
The sun surged toward the earth and the moon escaped from darkness
 to bless the union of two spirits so alike that your
Pain became my discomfort. In the hour when I stood naked,
 You were there to play the drum of life for us.

Beloved partner, keeper of my heart's odd secrets, clothed
 in summer blossoms so the icy hand of winter
Never touches us, I thank your patience. Our joining
 is like a tree to earth, a cloud to sky, and even more:
We are the reason the world can laugh on its battlefields
 and rise from the ashes of its selfishness to hear me say,
In this time, this place, this way, I loved you best of all.

Canyon Echoes

WHY THE GREAT SPIRIT MADE HANDS

The Great Spirit made hands before he made
    eyes or feet, so people could learn to hold
    one another. Hands were useful for touching
    the hard ribs of trees or the soft tongues of flower petals.
    Hands discovered the dry uncertainty of snakes, the
    slipperiness of fish, the mystery of feathers. Hands found
Other hands and clasped together to embrace the oncoming world,
    unafraid. Two pairs of hands, burned by fire and cooled
    by water, felt their way along unfamiliar paths and then
    reached out and found they needed one another
    to make a home in the wilderness of their minds.

Porcupine Winter

MARRIAGE RITUAL

When the earth was first made, all things were present,
    but people saw only their isolation from one another
    and from the mountains and the rivers that had created them.
For a long time, each creature followed a separate path, until
    the first man looked at the first woman and envisioned
    a unity not seen before. From their love, happiness was
Created and a thread soon connected man to woman, stars to trees,
    and the tongue of oceans to the thrust of rock. Some
    called it nature, others called it the plan of the universe.
But between men and women arose a bond of love, unbroken
    to the present day.

PARTNERS

On this day of sacred days, in this place of sacred places,
    You will become my dearest friend, my love,
    My partner on a life journey so rich and swift
    And memorable that the end of it will seem
But a moment from now. You and I are bound to give
    To one another the sacred love of generations
    Who stayed in the place of creation, forgetting
    The outside world in order to build from within.
Our marriage is a shrine to holy love, where the Creator
    placed everything of value for us to discover,
    the way our parents discovered their own world,
    and passed it on as witness to their loving time.

THE FOUR SISTERS OF
EVERLASTING BEAUTY

The Four Sisters of Everlasting Beauty danced on a mountaintop
in order to summon fire from deep within the earth. They
danced until flames poured from within veins in the rock,
cleansing them of selfishness and blame. The First Sister

Was the Dancing Woman of Mirth, whose direction was East. She wore
yellow, the color of awakening moments. She brought laughter,
the first necessity in a world of sadness. The First Sister said:
The spirit of laughter is the same as wind or water. It soothes

The troubled earth and makes hard edges disappear, even in the face of
sorrow. The Second Sister was the Woman of Long Experience,
whose direction was South. She wore blue, the color of memory.
She brought the imprint of fossils, also a collection of bones, the

Second necessity in a world filled with self-importance and envy. The
Second Sister said: The spirit of fossils and bones is the same as
long memory, a connection to the ancestors. It reminds the sick of health

And to the healthy gives warning of their mortality. The Third Sister
was the Woman of Unfulfilled Dreams, whose direction was West.
She wore red, the color of purpose and daring. She brought tears,
the third necessity in times when cleansing is required. The Third Sister

Residue

Said: The Spirit of weeping is nothing more than human rain, shed for loss
as well as love, and for children we never had. The unfulfilled
dreams of warriors and women, of birds taken from the nest, and of
animals denied their place in life, justify my gift of tears.

The Fourth Sister was the Retreating Woman of Consciousness, whose
direction was North. She wore white,
the color of beginning anew. She brought awareness, the fourth necessity
in a world of schemes and invention. The Fourth Sister said:
Honor yourself before all else and you will embrace
all life. All direction. All stars. All light.

And the other Three Sisters agreed.

Reunion

JOINED

Our connection to nature is nothing more
    than a deep conversation,
like that between two related stones or trees,
    an expanding bond of kinship
that sharpens perceptions and catches
    sunlight devouring ice on streams,
    a refrain of winter's resistance
To the unconditional surrender of spring.

Who knows the meaning behind a conversation
    between two partners of the soul,
so perfectly joined that they seem as natural
    as veins on leaves? Our connection
to nature is a magical cord that offers solace,
    granting us witness to the birth of stars.

Teton Cloud Dreamer

CHILDREN OF THE SUN

May you have life, my children of the sun. May you rise as smoke rises, and spread yourselves on the wind. In our house, you are always welcome. In our prayers, you will always hear your name spoken with reverence.

In you is the continuation of the world, both made and unmade. Soon you must go, for your roots are growing, and your branches are reaching out. Soon your wings must unfold, so you can stand at the edge of the cliff, learning

How to fly by yourself. You are free, my children of the sun, released from your familiar place. Our thoughts go with you. Our songs are sung for you. Our dances are intended to purify your heart. Please, now go.

ON CATCHING TIME

Once, when I was young, I attempted to catch time
    by nailing a spike to the moving shadow
    of the sun, which quickly passed
    from my command. Then I sought to catch

Time with a net of indifference, pretending one day was like
    another, but while my mind remained in summer,
    snowflakes fell. The matter of catching time absorbed

My attention as I raced ahead, only to find I couldn't
    catch time at all. In the shadow of my old age
    I find that time has caught up to me and I wish
    there were another summer left.

THE SHORTEST DAY /
THE LONGEST DAY

December 21

O sun, the father of us all, maker of ripe flowers, creator
    of fat corn, return this day to our part of the shrinking sky.
Your journey to the south is now complete and we pray to you
    to remember the drear, dark days of winter caught between
Your strong fingers struggling to release the earth from sleep. In this
    long gasp of icy silence, all creatures find renewal, a pale hope
That spring will not forget to come this year, nor will birds forget to lay eggs
    heavy with the yolk of generation.

June 21

Now the earth lies panting in the rich blood of summer, and you are content,
    O sun, father of full orchards and the restlessness of elk. We observe
Your deep shadows and hear the laughter of leaves green with continuity,
    but we are not deceived by the smoothness of our ripe landscape.
Even the longest day contains the seeds of winter and on the wind we hear
    the song that icicles sing to stay awake. The longest day is merely
A pause between the places where our lives are lived, and in its fullness
    we dance for the right of bumblebees to gather distant honey.

Chimayo Autumn

AUTUMN:
THE SWEEPING OF
MOTHER EARTH'S NAVEL

Thanks be to the Creator. Now in this time of harvest and plenty,
    we remember our connection to the earth. As she
    prepares to sleep, our work begins. At dawn, we sweep Mother Earth's
Navel, from which our prosperity comes. We leave offerings of corn and
    beans.
We embrace the departing birds and animals, also.

Blue River Sunset

THE RITUAL OF FORGETTING

When leaving one home and moving to another,
    The ancestors said goodbye to stale dreams.
They etched the rock with memory
    and mapped the way to change. The ancestors
Said goodbye to their village made of earth and to
    Shadows blurred by their own tears. They sang
The song of Ending and danced the Dance of Leaving,
    So nothing would be misunderstood
About the necessity to start again in a place of light
    They believed adjacent in their own hearts.

The ritual of forgetting took so long boys
    Grew into bears and girls became butterflies
While waiting for those old lines of place
    To disappear. The new village was the same
As the old village, except its edges were less rounded
    With sorrow, and along its walls slid the shadows
Of regret in which they saw old familiar pieces of themselves.
    The ritual of forgetting was the means by which
The ancestors prepared the ground for seeds of change,
    While remembering the tears required to grow them.

HOW TO BECOME A SNAKE

There are creatures on this earth which are not loved, among them snakes,
    who slide along the ground with forked tongues meant to carry messages
    of rain to those who believe in them. Among our people, men dance
With rattlesnakes, and hold them close to hear their words. We are not afraid,
    for to us those snakes are brothers, sharing their perspective of life
    lived close to the ground, without feet. Snakes are only meant to do
The work the Creator intended them to do. So why do people fear them?

GRIEF'S COMPANION: WAR

The death of children amidst the cross fire of ideas is evil's
    grandest gesture. Not even the loss of love nor a
    summer without flowers creates a grief as deep
As the theft of children's laughter. No horror speaks as loudly
    as the final cries of children, who, like birds,
    seek to spread their wings even when the sky bleeds
Dead dreams. In these dark moments, the Earth's great heart

Stops beating. In the void that evil leaves behind, a question
    arises: If fools make war on innocence,
    then who becomes grief's companion?

A single shaft of sunlight, falling on a drop of blood. A bird
    rising higher than danger. A blade of grass, defiantly green
    after fire wipes clean the face of desire. But most of all,
Music created by children's tears.

Old Walls

CHANGING

The life I shared with you was filled with flowers,
    but even flowers fade, as do rainbows
    and the smiles we used to share. Remember?

Our paths were joined for our chosen time
    and together we grew stronger than we
    would have grown alone. But now, my love,

I must go beyond this place we shared together,
    to a destination still unknown. My heart is
    filled with love and sorrow, joy and anticipation.

Our common journey taught us to value one another's causes,
    just as it opened the door to our individual claims. I do not
    love you less for deserting our common path, for the memory
of each step is what sustains me as I grope toward higher ground.
Oh, my love, I thank you for never letting go of my hand.

WHAT THE TREES SAID WHEN THEY FELL

The forest was an ancient tangle, so dense that whispers
    could not be heard between the leaves, so tall
That birds became caught in branches and never reached
    the sunlight, but spent their lives in the twilight
Layer where moss hung like ropes and the mist of ages
    clung thickly to the air. Trees grew like sentinels
To history, older than animals, birds, or fish ever dreamed
    of becoming when they were young and believed

That life would last forever. Those trees knew forever meant
    long centuries of observation of weather, birds,
And animals, also ferns and moss, the sliding nature of
    rocks embedded in mud and the temperament of snails.
Those trees grew up knowing all about one another, side by
    side in a moss-green light, comforted by wind trying
To get between them and by rain falling in vertical shafts
    anxious to penetrate their dry roots.

Those trees were necessary for balance, harmony, and beauty
    in the world. All the animals and birds knew their importance
And spent their days and nights honoring their existence. Then brazen
    people came and looked at the trees with calculating eyes.
They built roads and trails, then they cut them down, those ancient,
    peaceful ones.

The trees fell gracefully, according to their nature,
    one by one, with moans heard by birds and snails,
While in the river fish hid in dark pools. As the trees fell
    they said: We bore witness to our time and
Each of you shall bear witness to a different time. Then,
    where each tree fell, a child of destruction sprang up.

Lakota Blue Aura

SECRETS

After our land and names and ancient ways
    were ruined, the intruders wanted our secrets,
    the heart of a religion as old as stars,
    the means by which we connect ourselves
    to honeybees, yucca, and grizzly bears,
An umbilical cord among all things in the universe.

To each of us was given only part of the truth,
    like a branch of a very old tree, or
    a smooth stone flashing in the river,
    so that this sacred knowledge of birds
    and animals could not be sold for money,
Nor would we have had reason to think ourselves important.

The intruders never stopped to listen to anything
    except what they were determined to hear,
    the frantic stories we told to save ourselves
    from a destiny as inevitable as that of earth,
    which we alone remembered in her purity,
Craving her comfort in our time of desperation.

When they were satisfied, the intruders left our village
    and returned to their world, where they said:
    Secrets, that's what we learned back there.
    Secrets, to further scientific inquiry.
    Secrets, because it is our right to know
Even what is incomprehensible and therefore essential.

We told those intruders four centuries of intricate lies,
    drenched in deceptive sincerity, until they believed
    we had accepted the arrogance of their ways.
    They never knew that lies are often necessary
To the survival of honeybees, yucca, and grizzly bears.

Medicine

FATHER

Dear father of good example, man of few words,
    and tall, unwavering shadows, how do we,
    your children, offer thanks for your gifts

Of wisdom and bravery when others sought the safer route?
    Trying to walk in your footsteps, we became lost,
    just as our imitation of your presence brought us

Ridicule. We were not aware of your sacrifice and hard work
    on our behalf, nor did we understand your lessons,
    offered so the world would not drown us. Dear father,

Man among men, friend to those who were your enemies,
    and husband to a loving woman, we give you
    the universe reflected in our eyes.

WHEN I WAS YOUNG

Years ago, when I thought I would live forever, the thrust of youth
    seemed endless, like the sky expanding to hold my dreams.
    The path to knowledge was filled with expectation, yet
Disillusion blurred my eyes and in my sleep a holy man appeared

To warn me about life's treachery. When I was young, the world
    lay within my grasp, but I partook of folly just as I embraced youth's
    vanity. Now as old age wraps me in consideration of my end,
I rejoice in small things unnoticed until now when children's laughter

Becomes music of the deepest kind, and in the budding trees I find
    a thousand summers that I will never live to see. Now I am glad
    for the opportunity to share the lessons of my own time. Now
I know the mistakes of my foolish youth could not have been avoided.

MOTHER

On this day of days, this night of nights,
    we honor you, our mother of beauty
    and patience, who holds the light of
    generations between her hands.

From you comes the courage of women
    persisting in obscurity and the dreams of men
    caught in the dilemma of pursuit.
    The shape of meaning you forged

From scraps and out of fear you created hope.
    We honor your strength and enduring love,
    Mother of imperfect children, whose
    praises you sang because you loved us.

Your blood throbs with the pulse of cougars and bears,
    dead ancestors and extinct species, while in your womb
    lies the egg of mystery. Now, on this day of days,

We honor the courage of creation that is yours.

Canyon Lands

WISDOM OF THE ELDERS

Old Man Courage, look at you, dressed in your robe of experience,
Misunderstood by youth who believe themselves invincible.
    What can you tell them of the time in which they live?
        My words are of history and mistakes.
        My words are of the future and mistakes.
        Each is the same. Each is always ignored.
        Both history and future test one another, year after year.

Old Woman Patience, look at you, wearing a gown of reassurance,
Breathing between the blankets of despair, have you words for those
    Who never say thank you?
        My words are of stars, which held on tight.
        My words are of clouds, which never gave up.
        In wind, you will hear my song, year after year.
        In earth, you will find resistance forever.

But the two-legged creatures ignored the wisdom of the elders,
    and so they went away. Now you can hear them
    when the wind cries or the ocean roars, and in the forest,
    a tiny tree unfolds its perfect leaves.

Sarah Begay

MEDICINE WOMAN'S LESSON

What have I learned during this life of falling often on a path that
    offered me direction I did not take? The language of snails.

Why did I ignore the advice of those who had lived a long time?
    So that I could embrace my own mistakes.

Who was willing to accompany me on my painful journey?
    Myself alone, dragging along the shadows of experience.

What shall I give to those ready to embark upon an even steeper path?
    An open heart. Resistance to despair. Laughter. Most of all,

The love of birds, animals, and spirits who watched my progress and said,
    Though you have arrived, you are nowhere at all.

WINTER: LEANING TOWARD WARMTH

Silence is renewal. As earth sleeps under a blanket of peaceful snow,
    in our village we dream of life's endless circle. Leaning
    toward warmth in front of the fire, we remember how the seeds
Are sleeping, but in their hearts, full ears of summer corn begin to grow.

GRANDCHILDREN

In the eyes of grandchildren we see reflected
    our own forgotten youth, the dreams
    we had of greatness and bravery
    soon tamed by life's conflicting views.
How to spare grandchildren the pain of our mistakes?

In the laughter of grandchildren we hear the hope
    of every generation still fresh
    with anticipation, the kind that trees
    and melting snow bequeath to us each spring.
How to keep laughter from turning into tears?

Memory selects only the most enduring lessons
    to include in the great circle of life
    that neither wisdom nor generation
    can alter, no matter how great the effort.
Our grandchildren must have knowledge of their own time,
    and that is why we cannot spare them pain,
    nor can we trade their tears for laughter.

Phoenix Fire

DAYS OF THE SHORTEST SUN

The path of our elder the sun is a short path buried in the heart of winter,
    a time when certain animals and birds are marked for death
    the coming year. The ears of the animals are slit and some
Of the birds' feathers fall out. So too with humans who are marked
    for death in some way that only the spirits see. For four days we wait
    inside our houses, singing and drumming, wondering

Who will die and who will live. We attach ourselves to the sun's sash
    with pine gum, for we believe that this will keep us safe
    from illness and death the coming year. Even so, as our elder
The sun begins its journey to the north, it already knows which animals,
    which birds, and which humans are needed in the sky. So
    we wait for the long arms of the sun to embrace us,

Patiently, as the birds and the animals wait in their own way. When
    the days of the sun are shortest, our courage is longest, and our
    song is sweetest. We are able to hear the song of wild canaries
    in the snow, and on the bare branches plum blossoms bloom.

Teton Sentries

DEATH RITUAL

In Memoriam, Frank Waters

He died facedown, as if to observe the earth he came from and to understand
    at long last the fragility of life now over, yet this humble man
Of mountains and rivers, deep canyons and hard prairies believed
    his worth was in his immortal words, seized
    from the places that he loved.
Death was but another journey, and as he passed
    from one world to another,
    his voiceless voice was heard and his sightless eyes were made to see
Straight through this earth of ours, to stars yet unborn,
    and there he found rest,
    Awakening the universe with his song.

Touching Home

WHAT TO LEAVE BEHIND

The only gift to leave to children is example.
The only road to show them is awareness.
The only blessing to give them is responsibility.
The only thing to ask in return is understanding.
The only memory to take with you is one of love.

INDEX